Raymond Lotuaco DDS, Inc.
23501 Cinema Drive
Suite 207
Valencia, CA 91355

INSIDE

OUTSIDE

UPSIDE DOWN

INSIDE

OUTSIDE

UPSIDE DOWN

by Stan and Jan Berenstain

A Bright & Early Book

RANDOM HOUSE / NEW YORK

L M N O

Going in

Inside

Inside a box

Upside down

Inside a box
Upside down

Going out

Outside

Outside
Inside a box
Upside down

Going on

On a truck
Outside
Inside a box
Upside down

Going

Going to town
On a truck
Outside
Inside a box
Upside down

Falling off

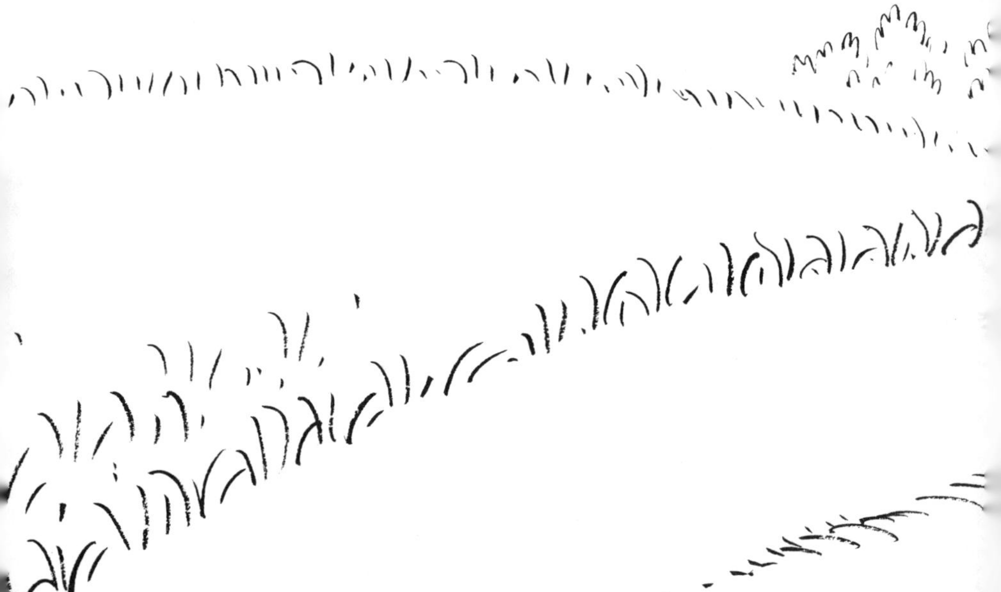

Off the truck

Coming out

Right side up !

Mama! Mama!
I went to town.
Inside,
Outside,
Upside down!